More Bermuda Rock Lessons

The Pond with No End

The Pond
with
No End

By Ezra Turner

Illustrated by Emma Ingham-Dounouk

ISBN: 1-894916-39-5

Published by Print Link
P.O. Box HM 937, Hamilton HM DX, Bermuda
Printed in Canada

Contents

Dedication

To my nephew, Jaki-da.
Many thanks to
Dr. Judy Hayward, Emma Ingham-Dounuk,
and Horst Augustinovic.

Spike

Spike's pond was beautiful and, to his little eyes, amazing. Many types of plant life surrounded it: mangrove and milkweed trees, duck grass and golden rod, which shone in the sunlight when it bloomed. Pebbles of various colours framed the water's edge, where nothing at all grew. When the sun hit these pebbles, they reflected all the colours of the rainbow. In the pond itself, the water changed constantly. If the wind blew hard, it streamed swiftly and raced over large boulders situated here and there in the pond, or else it cut through them, making channels. The pond was full of fish that swam with the current or hid in large plants that grew everywhere and swayed and bent with the water as it gushed by. Spike and other caterpillars that lived near him called their pond 'the pond with no end' because they had no idea where it led.

Spike belonged to a colony of caterpillars that were red, yellow or orange and sometimes had bristles that stuck out like little spears. The colourful colony made its home in an area of the pond that was full of milkweed trees that the caterpillars both lived in and feasted on. Typically, the caterpillars munched on the juicy leaves of the trees in the early morning, before the sun appeared on the horizon, and then took a nap.

Spike was a bright yellow caterpillar with black antennae poking out from either side of his head. Most days he spent his time watching the movement of the pond and the ducks that played in the grass around it. However, he had curious little mind that was full of questions. Sometimes these questions made him think for so long he would forget to eat and then his little belly would ache terribly. One morning Spike woke up determined to find answers to his questions. He decided he would crawl to the top of his milkweed tree and see what was what. If he couldn't find satisfaction there, he would go back down to the bottom and follow 'the pond with no end.' "Surely, there must be answers there!" he told himself, shouting out loud.

The caterpillars around Spike heard his outburst and woke up, wondering who or what was disturbing their rest. Rolling their eyes around, they saw Spike's bright yellow body lying across a milkweed leaf that looked particularly fleshy and appetizing. The caterpillars were ready for breakfast and the sight of the leaf made them hungry, but they were also interested to know what Spike was shouting about.

"Can anyone answer my question?" Spike cried.

At that a huge caterpillar shuffled his way through the others that were all bunched together along the leaves near Spike and asked, "What's the big question?"

Spike turned to the large caterpillar and said, "Where do we come from?"

The big caterpillar replied, "Everyone knows where we come from, Spike. We come from eggs."

The other caterpillars all started to laugh, which hurt Spike's feelings. He dropped his head and started to cry. The older caterpillar said, "Spike, there's no need to cry. You asked for an answer and you got it. Now are there any more questions?"

Spike raised his head and, wiping the tears from his eyes, said, "Where do the eggs come from?"

The caterpillars all started to laugh again. The big caterpillar ordered them to stop. Then he told Spike that no one knew where eggs came from. Hearing this, Spike asked, "Well, where do we go after we have eaten all the leaves on our milkweed trees?"

The caterpillars all gasped and looked uneasy. The large caterpillar wondered how a little one could have thought to ask such a question. He hesitated a bit and then spoke. "All I know is that after we have eaten and eaten we grow out of our skins. Then our bodies grow a new skin. After this has happened several times, we build a case around ourselves. Then we never eat or are seen again."

The idea of his skin splitting from his body seemed awful to Spike, who noticed that the other caterpillars seemed none too pleased about this either. He could also see that none of the caterpillars gathered around him had answers to his questions. Lifting his head high, he cried, "I am going to follow the pebbles beside 'the pond with no end' to search for the answers to my questions. I promise that when I find them I'll return and share my knowledge with everyone."

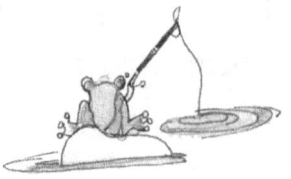

Duke the Frog

After Spike had made his promise, he began to crawl down the milkweed tree. As he made his way, some of the caterpillars he passed told him he should forget about his mission, while others just shook their heads sadly. Trying to ignore them, Spike blocked his ears and, taking deep breaths, continued on down towards the bottom of the milkweed tree. From there he would make his way through the tall grass to the pebbles beside the pond. He knew that once he reached these smooth stones his journey would become easier and faster.

Spike's little feet had never touched grass before, and his first encounter with it sent a chill right through his body. "Yuck," he said, pausing before attempting to take another step. Getting through the tall grass wasn't going to be what he had imagined. From his milkweed tree, it had looked as though it wouldn't be difficult at all. Now he asked himself, "How in the world will I make it through this mess?" But although it was dark, cold and lonely, he was determined. He would persevere, taking one step at a time.

Spike didn't get too far before he heard a loud quack, which seemed to come from nowhere. Startled, he glanced from side to side, seeing nothing. Then, looking behind him, he spotted a sly-looking duck that wouldn't have seemed nearly so frightening from his milkweed tree as it did right now. The duck peered down at Spike and began to jerk its head back and forth, as if it were getting ready to dart down and gobble him up. But then, just in time, a big yellow creature popped up between Spike and the duck, which became so scared it flapped its wings, turned around and quickly waddled away.

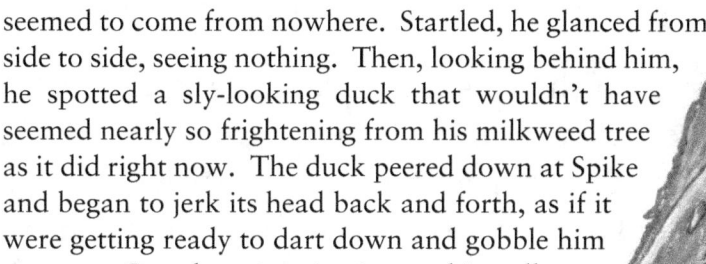

Spike thanked his unknown rescuer and sighed, "I thought I was a goner."

The newcomer took several deep breaths, which were followed by loud croaking noises that seemed to rise up from its throat, and said, "What's your name?"

"Spike!" declared the little caterpillar.

Then the stranger asked, "What brings you to these parts? I've never seen anything like you before."

Spike replied, "I'm a caterpillar who comes from an egg and will eat so much my body will outgrow its skin. The only time I'll

5

stop eating is when my skin splits." With a tear in his eye, Spike continued, "After my skin splits several times, I'll build a case around myself and then I'll never be seen again."

The stranger laughed and said, "Don't be so hard on yourself."

Spike was grateful that his life had been saved, but he could not forget that he was on a mission to find answers. His rescuer, powerful as he might be, did not have them. So Spike thanked his lifesaver and said, "I must be going now." He set off through the tall grass, which seemed to be getting more and more difficult to crawl through. Trudging forward, he turned around only when he heard a familiar croak coming from behind him. Within a second, the source of the noise had hopped right up beside him. Peering down, the creature gave a wide smile and said, "My name is Duke the Frog. I like your courage and if you don't mind I'd like to help you." Croaking again, the frog said, "I'm quick, and you sure won't have to worry about being eaten by ducks. I'll protect you."

Spike looked up into Duke's big bulging eyes and thought for a moment before saying, "Okay, but I can't pay you for helping me."

"That's okay, kid," Duke said. Then he squatted down and let Spike crawl up on him, waiting until the caterpillar had found a comfortable place on top of his head. "So, where to now, kid?" the frog asked.

"We're going to the pebbles alongside the pond. It will be easier to follow the pond from there," Spike replied.

Duke began to hop and the new partners started singing, "Away we go through the duck grass and golden rod to the beautiful pebbles by 'the pond with no end.'" When they reached the edge of the pond, Spike slid off Duke's head in a hurry. He couldn't wait to feel the beautiful pebbles he had imagined touching for so long.

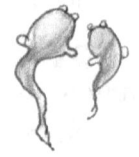

Steven

hen Spike's small feet landed on the pebbles, he found that they were warm, not cold and clammy like the soil underneath the grass. He began crawling all over them, laughing with joy. Brimming with confidence, he told himself that since he had reached the pebbles, he was sure he would have no trouble following the `pond with no end' to find answers to his questions.

Meanwhile, Duke decided he was thirsty and hopped over to the edge of the pond. While he was drinking, a little fish-like creature raised its head out of the water, blew bubbles in his eyes and swam off, laughing. This upset Duke so much that he began to croak loudly. The noise startled Spike, so he crawled over to see what was wrong. Spike knew Duke was perturbed when he saw his new friend's throat blow out like a big balloon. "What's the matter Duke? You don't look so good," he said.

Duke began to release air and, as he gave a loud croak, his throat returned to normal. In a grouchy voice, he complained, "A little fish just blew bubbles in my eyes and swam off laughing. If I could get my tongue on him, he wouldn't do it again." Spike tried not to giggle, but his little body swelled up as he tried to hold back the laughter. Things got even funnier when the little fish popped his head out of the water and declared, "I'm not a fish. I'm a tadpole."

"At least he knows who he is!" Spike shouted to Duke. Turning to the tadpole, he said, "So, what's your name?"

"Steven," the tadpole replied, blowing more bubbles.

"Where do you come from?" Spike asked.

Steven thought for a while and said, "I come from an egg."

Duke asked, "Where does the egg come from?"

Steven looked puzzled, so Spike said, "Don't worry. No one knows that. You could join us on our journey to the end of the pond if you want to find the answer."

Steven opened his eyes wide and exclaimed, "That's forbidden. No one who has tried to follow the pond has ever returned."

Spike interrupted him, saying, "We know that. But it's better to try, whatever the cost." Crawling up onto Duke's head, he made himself comfortable between the frog's two large eyes. Duke began to hop along the pebbles, following 'the pond with no end.'

"Hey!" screamed Steven, who began swimming

9

towards them. When he reached the pair, he stuck his head out of the water and said, "Can I join you?"

Looking down from Duke's head, Spike replied, "If you want to know where you came from and where you are going, you surely can."

Steven blew a line of bubbles that went way up into the sky. "Okay," yelled Duke, "Now it's a caterpillar, a frog and a tadpole." Leading them in a song, he croaked, "Along we go. A highway of beautiful pebbles is our path as we follow `the pond with no end, no end.'"

"No end," squealed Steven, out of tune.

Spike began counting the different colours of the pebbles. But there were so many he couldn't figure out how many were green or yellow or blue. To make matters worse, he had to turn his bright yellow neck from side to side and backward and forward as Duke hopped. He not only lost count but also got a stiff neck. Finally, he decided he would count each time Duke hopped. So every time Duke leapt, he hollered out a number, while Steven blew a bubble and said "one bubble, two bubbles" and so on.

10

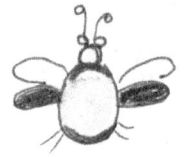

The Little
Black Creatures

After Spike had counted out fifty hops, Duke stopped and said he was hungry. At the same time, he began sucking in his breath and, as he did so, his throat started to expand. Spike thought he was angry, for this was what Duke had done when Steven blew bubbles in his face. Craning his neck to look into his friend's big eyes, Spike asked, "Did I do something to make you mad,, Duke?" There was no reply. After trying several more times to get a response from Duke, the caterpillar slid down his friend's back and leg onto his webbed foot and started over to the pond.

When Spike arrived at the edge of the pond, he saw Steven in the water, chewing away on a plant that was swaying slowly with the current and then straightening itself out, only to bend again. Steven, who was following the plant's twists and turns, seemed to be having a great time. Suddenly, Spike's little ears began to hum. He turned to see where the sound was coming from and noticed a number of little black specks flying around Duke's throat. He became worried, thinking the creatures might be trying to hurt the frog. He was just about to shout out and try to scare the little pests away, when he saw Duke's tongue dart out of his mouth and catch four of them at once. As he continued to watch, Duke's tongue returned to his mouth and his balloon throat rolled over. Relaxing, Spike looked on silently as Duke proceeded to catch more of the creatures, until only seven were left.

Spike began to count. "One, two, three, four with one lick of the tongue," he said softly. Then Duke's tongue flew out again and caught more little creatures. "Five, six, seven. Now there are no more black creatures left," Spike said.

Duke let out a loud burp and his balloon throat began to retract. With a croaky voice he said, "Sorry for not answering you kid, but when I'm eating I have to be very quiet."

Spike asked, "What were those little black things?"

Duke grinned and said, "They're called flies."

"Are they as tasty as my milkweed leaves?" Spike asked.

"Just as good and even better," Duke replied.

Spike wondered about that. Nothing could be as good as his milkweed leaves. Just the thought of them

12

made his stomach growl. He remembered that he hadn't eaten anything since sunrise that morning. Now he yearned to sink his teeth into a fleshy leaf.

Duke noticed Spike daydreaming and asked, "Do you want me to catch you a fly?"

Spike shook his head and said, "No thank you. I'm not hungry."

Duke replied, "I haven't seen you eat anything all day."

"I'm not hungry!" Spike insisted, his black antennae shaking and sticking out like spears.

Steven poked his head up out of the water and said, "Are we going to sleep here tonight? Because if we are I'm going to make myself a bed in the plants."

Duke said, "I'm a little tired myself. How about you, kid?"

By now, Spike's little antennae were almost covering his eyes. He said, "Yes, I think we've traveled enough for one day."

Hearing those words, Steven said goodnight and swam down between the plants. Duke crouched low and spread out his front legs, giving Spike room to nestle between his two webbed feet.
Feeling comfortable and safe, Spike
said goodnight to Duke, who
was already asleep.

Something That Goes
Hiss in the Night

Spike began to watch the day change into night, just as he had done many times back on his milkweed tree. His little eyes grew heavy as he looked at the sunset, and at the water of the pond changing color. He knew that the last day bird was hurrying to find a safe, warm place for the night. He also knew that while the daytime had been busy with creatures playing, eating and swimming, the night would soon come to life too. Once it got dark, creatures that slept when the sun was up would awake to do the same things as the day crowd.

Spike was about to fall asleep when he heard several whooping noises. He opened his droopy eyes to see two owls flying from the tall trees. He was not afraid of owls. He had watched them from his milkweed tree on many a night. But tonight the wise birds seemed to be signaling that something was different. Spike felt anxious and, to make matters worse, his stomach really ached now. He knew he had to eat something. Silently, moving one of his little legs at a time, he crawled out from beneath Duke's webbed toes, being careful not to wake the frog. Free, Spike inched over to the pond. Looking into it, he saw the reflection of the stars twinkling on the water's surface. Fireflies had lit up the pond like a Christmas tree. But Spike's aching stomach wouldn't let him enjoy the moment. With hunger guiding him, he crawled over the pebbles alongside the pond to a golden rod bush.

When Spike got to the bush, his mouth started to water and he couldn't wait to sink his teeth into the fat leaves. He knew what would happen if he ate too much, but he chewed and chewed until he felt his belly swelling up like Duke's throat. He was just forcing his mouth open to take one more bite when he heard a loud hissing sound, followed by rustling leaves. Spike knew that whatever was making the noise had to be huge, so he sat very still. The swishing sound got louder and louder, until out from under a bush slid a big snake that kept on slithering

until it was right in front of Spike. Then the snake stuck out its tongue and gave a loud hiss. Spike shut his eyes and shivered.

At about the same time, Spike heard a familiar croak come from over near the pond. The snake's neck did a quick u-turn and its tongue pointed in the direction of the sound. It began to zigzag across the pebbles towards the noise. When it reached Duke, the frog leapt over the snake and headed back towards Spike. "Hurry up and climb aboard," Duke told the little caterpillar. But every time Spike tried to crawl onto Duke's back, he fell off again onto the pebbles. His eyes filling up with tears, Spike cried, "Duke, I can't move. I ate too much."

By now, the snake was back on the trail, hissing louder than ever. By instinct, Duke stuck his tongue out towards Spike. Picking the little caterpillar up, he tipped him backwards and then flicked him off his tongue onto his head. Spike was now staring right into the snake's eyes! "Hurry, Duke," he shouted. Hopping as high as he could, Duke jumped over the snake and then made several more good hops before the creature guessed what was happening. But the two friends could not shake the snake, which continued to follow them along the pebbles, all the while making the hissing sound that sent chills down Spike's antennae. "Don't stop. Keep going, Duke!" Spike screamed.

Duke hopped over to the edge of the pond and hollered, "Hold your breath!" He jumped into the pond with the determined snake slipping into the water behind them. Luckily, Duke spotted a boulder protruding out of the water and clung on to it with his webbed feet. Hidden, he watched the snake swoosh by. Duke waited until it was out of sight and then climbed slowly to the top of the boulder. Taking a deep breath, he made one big hop to the pebbles. After the pair had landed on the stones, Spike slid off Duke's head. He was as round as a ball from all the food and water he had taken in and almost rolled back into the pond. Just in time, Duke stuck out one of his webbed feet to stop him.

Duke looked down at Spike and hardly recognized him. He could only tell who it was by the black antennae, which were standing out like spears. "Kid, are you okay?" the frog asked. When Spike didn't answer, Duke pressed gently on the caterpillar's soft, squishy body. Water came spurting out of Spike's mouth and, after several more presses, he began to look like his old self. There was just a little bulge in his stomach from all the leaves he had devoured.

Slowly, Spike began to breathe comfortably again. After he had taken several deep breaths, he raised his little head and stared into Duke's big eyes, which looked as though they were about to pop out. "I'm okay Duke. But I feel a little weak," Spike murmured.

Duke rolled his eyes from side to side, making sure the coast was clear and everything was safe. Then, he smiled at his friend and said, "Close your eyes and rest." Feeling safe once again, Spike closed his eyes. Soon he was fast asleep and Duke was right behind him, following him to dreamland. As the two slept, the night ticked away.

Soft Eyes

When the first light crept up over the horizon, fish began swimming around in the pond and the day birds began to wake up, starting with the redbird, who was an alarm clock for the others. Soon all the birds struck up a chorus and one voice couldn't be distinguished from another. Only an experienced ear could tell who was singing which tune.

One by one, ducks began stretching their necks out of the tall grass to greet the morning sun. Their ducklings began clamoring for food. The older ducks flapped

their wings and trotted across the pebbles to the pond, the ducklings trailing behind in single file. After making sure the young ones were alright, the mother ducks quacked and paddled off into the water in search of fish to eat. Their ducklings knew enough to do the same.

Steven also woke up with the morning sun. Giving his body a little shake, he swam out from between the plants to the top of the water. Popping his head up, he blew a line of bubbles that went high up in the air and burst, one after another. He called out, "Duke, Spike. Time to get up!" There was no answer. Steven glanced across the pebbles, but he saw no sign of his two friends. Poking his head further out of the water, he shouted, "This is no time for games." Steven still didn't hear any familiar voices. How could he have known that while he slept a huge snake had chased Duke and Spike?

Steven's eyes watered and he began to wonder if Duke and Spike had abandoned him, after promising he could join them in their search for answers. Steven began to feel alone and afraid. He wanted to go back to the safety of the plants he knew and had left behind. Turning around, he looked back towards where he had come from. But home was nowhere in sight and seemed far away. He dove back down into the pond and started to cry. His tears made bubbles on the surface of the water and drew the attention of two soft eyes that had been

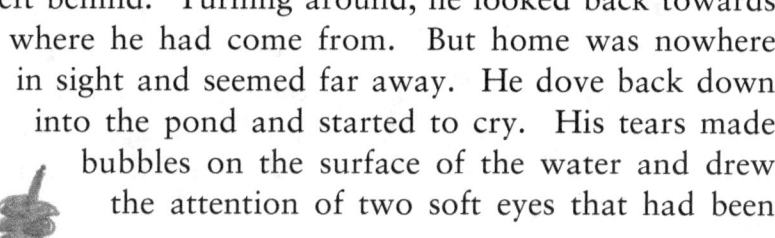

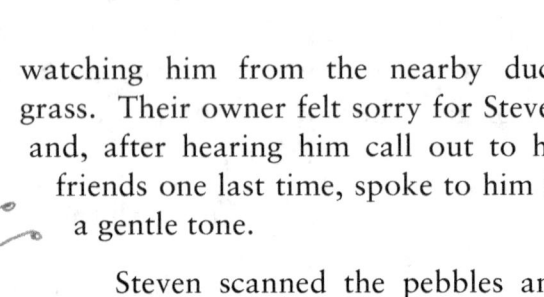

watching him from the nearby duck grass. Their owner felt sorry for Steven and, after hearing him call out to his friends one last time, spoke to him in a gentle tone.

Steven scanned the pebbles and cried, "Spike is that you?"

Then Steven heard a voice say "Sorry little fellow. Did you lose your parents?"

Steven didn't answer because he couldn't tell where the voice was coming from. Then he looked towards the duck grass and was afraid, at first, when he discovered the source. Never before had he seen anything so beautiful. His little body froze as he gazed at the spectacle. He saw wings spread out to capture all the rays of the sun. The colours on display seemed magical. Steven was still in a trance when the gorgeous creature flew off the duck grass in his direction. It landed on an orange-colored pebble next to the pond, looked at him and said, "Are you lost?"

Almost speechless, Steven somehow managed to tell how he had joined Duke and Spike in their search for answers. When he had finished the whole story, the lovely creature with soft eyes said, "My name is Psyche. I'm a butterfly. If you wish, I can help you find your friends."

The little tadpole interrupted her, saying, "Friends? Huh, not anymore. Friends don't leave their so-called friends behind. They're not my friends anymore and when I find them I'm going to give them a piece of my mind."

Psyche said, "Don't be so quick to judge. Wait until you find out what really happened. Who knows, maybe they were chased by one of the night hunters."

Steven cooled down a bit and said, "You might be right. I hope nothing has happened to my friends."

"Let's hope not," replied Psyche. Smiling, she said, "Well, we're not helping by sitting here."

And so, the butterfly and the tadpole began their search for the caterpillar and the frog.

Jell-O

urther down the pond, Duke was nestled amongst the pebbles, where he had slept away most of the delightful morning. When he finally woke up, the sun was high in the sky and shining so brightly it took him a second or two to adjust his eyes. When he was able to focus, Duke looked between his webbed front feet for Spike. All he saw was a patch of red pebbles where the caterpillar had been.

Duke's heart began to beat faster as he wondered what had happened to his friend while he had been sleeping. He hopped to the edge of the pond and called Spike's name, only to hear the echo of his own voice come back. Then, behind a green pebble, he spotted something yellow. Hopping over to it, he said, "Hey, you gave me a scare!" But when he looked closer, Duke couldn't believe his eyes. There, behind the pebble, was Spike's skin, bright yellow and lifeless. Tears began to form in his big bulging eyes. He was half croaking and half crying when he heard a faint voice calling his name. Turning his head quickly, Duke noticed a pair of small antennae sticking out from behind another pebble. Relieved, he started to hop over to the pebble.

But Spike stopped the frog in his tracks, shouting, "No! Don't come any closer, Duke."

"Why not?" responded Duke.

"Because I don't have any skin!" exclaimed Spike.

Rolling his eyes around and around, Duke said, "What happened?"

The little caterpillar replied, "Remember what I said happens to caterpillars when they eat too much, that their skins split because their bodies outgrow them?"

Duke thought for a moment and said, "Yes I remember you saying that, but I never took you seriously. I thought you were just upset and putting yourself down." He began hopping towards Spike again. But the little caterpillar pulled his antennae in behind the pebble even further and begged him not to come closer. Ignoring the plea, Duke said, "It can't be that bad." But when he reached the pebble Spike was hiding behind, he looked down and gasped. He couldn't believe his eyes. His friend's bright yellow body was now green and transparent. It looked just like Jell-O.

Duke's heart sank. He couldn't have imagined it would be this bad. He asked Spike if there was anything he could do for him, but Spike just shook his head and shut his eyes, trying to stop the tears from rolling down his face. Duke placed his big webbed feet on either side of Spike and lowered his head over his friend to protect him from the sun. The two stayed like that throughout the day.

Psyche to the Rescue

Meanwhile, Steven and Psyche were still searching for Duke and Spike. It was getting late and the sun was beginning to set. The butterfly flapped her wings and said, "We might have to sleep here for the night."

Steven pleaded, crying, "Please! Not yet! Let's keep going until the sun goes below the tip of the tall trees."

Fluttering her wings, Psyche sighed, "Okay Steven."

The two continued their journey, with Steven swimming and Psyche hovering above him. After a while, without warning, the water started to churn and splash. Little fish began to jump high out of the water. They were trying to escape bigger fish, hoping not to become their next meal. Praying he wouldn't be noticed, Steven hid behind some plants, while Psyche perched on a nearby pebble and looked on with concern. As the excitement continued, one big fish separated from the others and went over to the plant where Steven was hiding. Discovering Steven, it began making moves to eat him. Desperate to escape, Steven swam round and round in circles and soon became very tired.

The big fish closed in, until the tiny tadpole was only a mouthful away from being gobbled up. In one fast motion, Psyche flapped her wings and dove down towards the fish. With her wings extended, she looked like a bird. The fish was about to close its jaws on Steven when it saw Psyche and noticed the two round eyes patterned on each of her wings. Quickly, it turned and swam off in the opposite direction.

Steven's small heart was pounding rapidly when he popped his head out of the water to thank Psyche. The sun was now sinking below the tips of the tall trees and Psyche said, "Let's sleep here." Steven agreed. They said goodnight and Psyche flitted to the top of the nearby duck grass. Folding her wings close together, she settled in for the night. But Steven began to toss and turn between the plants. He couldn't get comfortable, and his mind was jumping from one thought to another. One minute he was mad at Spike and Duke and the next minute he was sad. Had something happened to them? He didn't know what to think. The little tadpole's eyes stayed open as he watched the day turn into night and heard the last cries of the day creatures.

Soon, like magic, the stars came out and the pond was once again lit up with fireflies. Then followed the whooping of the owls. Just like the redbirds in the morning, the owls sounded the alarm for the night crew to get up. Before long, Steven's eyes became too heavy to keep open and he drifted off to dreamland.

The Biggest Hop Ever

The next morning, at the first peep of the sun, the night creatures raced to find a place where they could sleep safely through the day. At the same time, the day shift came on and its creatures stretched their necks, wings and legs to greet the morning. Soon, the redbirds began to lead everyone in song and before long a whole band was playing.

Duke awoke to the sound of shouting and laughter. He saw Spike rolling over on the pebbles. The little caterpillar seemed full of life. Duke noticed that his friend had grown a new skin overnight and broke out into a big smile. He gave a loud croak and held his breath. As he did so, his throat began to expand and a dim light began blinking on and off inside it. Seeing all this, Spike stopped rolling around to watch. When Duke gave another loud croak, he was startled and jumped, pulling in his new spring body. But then before his eyes, Duke released the air in his throat and it returned to normal size. Grinning, Duke said, "It looks like you're ready to continue your journey."

Spike replied, "Yes, I'm as ready as ready can be."

Spike crawled over to Duke and climbed onto his webbed feet, continuing until he reached the center of his friend's head, between the frog's big eyes. He was about to give Duke the signal to start hopping when he noticed tiny bubbles forming on the surface of the pond. Shouting, Spike called, "Steven is that you?" There was no reply and after several attempts Spike stopped calling and began to cry.

Duke rolled his eyes upward and said, "Kid, there's nothing you can do."

Spike's antennae shot out and he shouted, "We promised Steven he could join us and we have deserted him." Wiping his eyes, he continued, "He must be lonely and very sad."

Duke rolled his eyeballs around in a circle and said, "Kid, we can't stop fate. We had to save ourselves from the snake." Then he rolled his eyes up toward Spike and said, "If that little tadpole has a bit of sense he'll continue flowing with the pond and hope fate leads him to us."

Spike's antennae relaxed and drooped down to cover his eyes. He smiled and said, "You're right. Let's continue our journey."

Duke began to hop and Spike began counting Duke's jumps out loud, hoping Steven would hear him. Eventually, Duke stopped and said, "Let's stay here for the rest of the day." Before Spike could answer, he heard a loud croak. It sounded just like Duke but was coming from a nearby bush. Duke began to scout around, looking for the source of the noise. A bit concerned, Spike asked, "What's that?" Duke told him to be quiet as the croaking got even louder. Then the bush began to move and the source of the mysterious croaking began to appear out in the open. Spike shrieked, crying, "It's another snake!"

"Be quiet!" Duke ordered. "It's not a poisonous snake but something that can be just as dangerous."

Hearing this, Spike trembled and pulled in his spring body, which was now twice the size his body had been when he left his milkweed tree. The bush started rustling even louder and soon a frog hopped out from among its leaves. Upon seeing the newcomer, Spike smiled and said, "It's not a snake Duke. It looks just like you."

Duke whispered, "What is it doing?"

Spike replied, "It's hopping right towards us."

With that, Duke lifted his head quickly and made the biggest hop ever, even bigger than the one he had made when they were being chased by the snake. Spike had to hold on with all of his little feet to keep from falling off. The frog was right behind, following them with even more determination than the snake.

You're Not Like Us

While this chase was taking place, Steven and Psyche had been continuing their search for Spike and Duke. Every now and then, Steven had raised his head from the water and shouted, "Duke. Spike." There was never any reply. At one point, Psyche decided to fly over to the tall grass that bordered the pond to look for signs of the frog and caterpillar. All she saw was a baby duckling wobbling out of the grass. When she returned to the pond, Steven had disappeared. Psyche began to shout his name but all that came back was her own echo. How could she have known that while she had been looking for Spike and Duke near the duck grass, Steven had swum down the pond and become lost?

Down 'the pond with no end,' where in the past he had been forbidden to go, Steven came across several little tadpoles playing a game. He had always thought that all the tadpoles in the world came from where he was from, but here was a whole new colony. Amazed, he wondered if they were for real. Then he began to wonder if they were friendly. Suddenly, he heard one of them shout, "I told you I saw someone."

"What is it?" inquired another, adding "Let's ask."

Then the first little tadpole said, "My name is Jane. What's your name?"

"Steven," replied the outsider.

"He can talk," Jane cried. Then she said, "What are you? I'm a tadpole."

All of the tadpoles looked at each other in disbelief. Poor little Steven had no idea of how much he had changed. Finally, Jane broke the silence and asked, "Do you want to play with us?"

Steven's eyes shone. He was so happy to have new friends, especially ones that were tadpoles who wanted to have fun like him. Spike and Duke only wanted to waste their time looking for silly answers. Steven said yes gladly and they all played together for the remainder of the day and had lots of fun.

As the sun began to set, the tadpoles went down in between the leaves of a huge plant. Steven swam down to join them, but Frank, Jane's oldest brother, stopped him. "Steven," he said, "we had fun playing with you but you can't sleep with us."

Steven looked puzzled and said, "But I thought we were friends."

"Steven, you're not like us," Frank replied.

"What do you mean?" asked Steven, more confused than ever.

"Can't you see," laughed Tim, the youngest tadpole brother. "You're not a tadpole. Look at those little web-like feet you have. And you don't have a tail."

All the tadpoles began to laugh, except Jane. But there wasn't a thing she could do. Her brothers were right, Steven wasn't like them at all. Steven turned slowly and sadly swam away. When he had gone some distance from the tadpoles, he went behind a plant and peered down to examine his tiny webbed feet. Looking back to where his tail had been, he noticed that there was only a stub now. He felt overwhelmed and tears began to stream from his eyes. He couldn't understand what was happening to him.

Sue

Meanwhile, Duke was moving as fast as he could with the new frog gaining ground with every hop he made. With Spike on his head, Duke soon grew tired and his leaps became shorter and shorter, until finally he collapsed. "Aha! I've caught you!" shouted the new frog, jumping right up to Duke and not noticing Spike until the caterpillar stood up on his hind legs and stuck out his black antennae. Yelling at the top of his voice, Spike cried, "Don't you touch my friend!"

The new frog looked surprised and said, "I want no fight with you. My fight is with Duke."

Spike said, "How do you know Duke's name?"

The new frog gave a little laugh and answered, "Who doesn't." Continuing, the newcomer said, "Your so-called friend and I used to be very close until one day he left without saying a word. I haven't laid eyes on him since and want some answers, like why he left."

Spike peered down at Duke and asked, "Is this true?" Without answering, Duke dropped his head in shame and Spike realized the new frog was telling the truth. Spike lowered his antennae and, before lying back on Duke's head, said, "I'm sorry."

"No need to be sorry," replied the new frog. "You were only protecting your so-called friend."

By now, the sun had set and the first star had appeared. Before long, the sky was twinkling with stars and the new frog, whose name was Sue, was telling Spike all about Duke and his cunning ways. Spike, who was beginning to like Sue, listened with amazement as the frog also told him about her own adventures. His eyes were drooping and starting to close, but he forced them open, wanting to stay awake so he could hear every word. But before long both he and Sue drifted off to sleep.

Spike awoke early the next morning and found Duke already up and waiting for him. Duke told him to climb aboard and hold his breath. Then he leapt into the pond, leaving Sue behind, asleep. Duke pushed his hind legs backwards and forwards, swimming underwater as fast as he could, not stopping until he knew Sue would be out of sight. At the end of the swim, Spike rolled off Duke's head and bounced up and down on the pebbles, water spurting out of his mouth with every bounce. Eventually, Duke stopped him with one of his feet and gently pressed out the remaining water.

Spike gasped for air and, when fully recovered, asked Duke, "Why did you leave Sue behind? She only wanted to talk to you." Duke didn't answer, so Spike shouted, "Just because you don't get your own way you leave." Flashing his black antennae from side to side, Spike stood up on his hind legs. He had grown much bigger and could now look Duke straight in his huge eyes. Facing him, Spike said, "What are you going to do now, desert me too? Well, go right ahead." Then he pointed his finger, instructing Duke to leave. Slowly, Duke turned in the opposite direction and hopped off. Only when he was out of sight did Spike break down and cry. Big teardrops rolled down his fat cheeks and fell in between two blue pebbles, where they made a small puddle.

34

Everything Changes

Steven, who had gone off to find his own bed after the other tadpoles had rejected him, slept late the following morning. He was awakened by the sound of someone calling his name. Opening eyes that were still sore from crying himself to sleep, Steven swam out from between the plants he had settled into the night before and poked his head up out of the water. There was Psyche, perched on a branch sticking up out of the pond. "Psyche!" he shouted, swimming as fast as he could in her direction. Upon seeing Steven, Psyche spread her shimmering wings. Her mouth dropped open, but no words came out. Instead, tears poured from her eyes. "Please don't cry," Steven begged. But the more he pleaded, the more Psyche wept, stopping only when she saw Steven plopping one of his newly-webbed feet up onto her branch.

When Steven had climbed right up next to her, Psyche wiped away her tears, smiled and said, "I thought a big fish had eaten you and I blamed myself for leaving you alone. You see Steven, my tears are tears of joy at seeing you."

Smiling back, Steven told her about how he had met some tadpoles that at first had played with him but then had teased him and chased him away because he was different from them.

Psyche tried to comfort Steven, explaining that everything changes in time and that some day those tadpoles would change too. Then they wouldn't think it was so funny, she told him. Regaining confidence, Steven made a big hop into the pond and blew a line of bubbles high into the sky. After a while, Psyche flew off her branch to join him and together the two resumed their search for Spike and Duke.

As Psyche was flying along above Steven, something bright yellow on the ground caught her eye. Looking down at the tadpole, she asked, "Didn't you say that your friend Spike was yellow?"

"Yes," replied Steven.

Psyche said, "Well, I see something yellow between the pebbles. I'm going to fly over to take a closer look. You stay right here where I can see you."

When she reached the yellow object that was lying on the ground, Psyche discovered that it was only an empty skin. Going back to tell Steven, she said, "It looks like Spike's gone. The only thing left is his skin." Wanting to see for himself, Steven climbed out of the pond onto the pebbles and took little hops over to Spike's discarded skin. "I'm sorry," Psyche said. But Steven just smiled. Surprised, Psyche wondered how he could be pleased to see his friend reduced to such a state.

"Don't be sad," Steven said. Then he explained what Spike had told him would happen if he ate too much.

"You mean that he has grown a new skin?" Psyche asked.

"Yes," replied Steven. "This will happen several times and then he'll build a case around himself."

Psyche interrupted him, exclaiming, "That means we don't have much time!"

"We have enough time to find him," Steven replied. And so, the pair started out again on their search.

37

My Best Friend

Further down 'the pond with no end,' Spike, who no longer had Duke to carry him, was finding it difficult to drag himself along the pebbles. When the sun began to set on another long day, he came across a bush that looked tempting and began to munch uncontrollably on its leaves. After he had stuffed himself, Spike fell asleep, only to wake up the next day and find that his skin had split from his body again. This meant he would have to hide under a leaf to avoid the hot sun. That night, when it got cold, he would need to find another leaf he could curl up in to keep warm.

Before the sun had risen too high, Spike laid down on a purple pebble to watch some ducklings play in the pond. He noticed how one little bird would peck another and swim off in the opposite direction. The first duckling's victim would then chase him down, peck him back and swim away himself. After that, the game would start up again, the action repeating itself. Spike was looking on with fascination when he heard loud croaking behind him. He turned quickly and shouted Duke's name, only to find out it wasn't Duke. Instead of his yellow-skinned friend, he saw a huge green frog glaring down at him. Spike tried to crawl away, but the frog hopped in front of him and, in a threatening tone, demanded, "Where do you think you're going?"

"I'm on a mission, looking for answers to my questions," Spike replied.

"So you are," said the frog, "but you're not going anywhere until I have a little fun with you first."

Spike couldn't imagine why the frog wanted to have fun with him since they weren't even friends, so he shifted around a bit and said, "I'm sorry but I don't have time for games." Spike tried to crawl past the big green frog but the creature stuck out a large webbed foot, put it on him and began to squeeze down on his soft little body. Spike pulled himself in and cried, "Stop that! It hurts!" The big green frog just laughed and kept on squeezing, until Spike began to feel quite sore. He started to cry, but the big green frog just laughed and kept on squishing.

It only stopped pressing when it heard a croak that was unfamiliar and turned around to find itself face to face with Duke, who shouted, "Don't you lay another foot on my friend!"

The big green frog laughed even louder and said, "This worm belongs to me."

Duke shouted back, "He's not a worm, he's a caterpillar and he's my best friend."

"Your friend? I've never heard such nonsense," the green frog retorted, starting to whistle. As it did so, three huge frogs hopped out of the duck grass and landed beside it. Looking at them, the green frog pointed one of its webbed feet at Duke and said, "This yellow frog is trying to steal my worm."

One of the newcomers looked into Duke's eyes and in a firm voice said, "You must leave now."

"Not without my friend," replied Duke, pointing at Spike.

The first green frog's throat began to expand and it raised a large webbed foot to strike Duke. But suddenly it froze, hearing a familiar voice behind it. "Don't you dare touch him!" the voice shouted. All the frogs turned around at once and found themselves face to face with none other than Sue. Without even a backward glance, they fled, leaving Spike and Duke behind. From that day forward, Duke's feelings for Sue changed and his big eyes developed a twinkle. Spike, overjoyed to see them together and happy, would take turns riding on each of their heads.

More Questions

One day Sue wasn't feeling well and spent the whole day in the pond as Duke sat at the water's edge and watched her with concern. From behind a pebble, Spike noticed Duke looking worriedly at Sue and crawled over to him. Lying beside one of Duke's webbed feet, he looked up and asked, "What's wrong with Sue?"

"She's sick," Duke answered.

"Did she eat too much?" Spike questioned.

"Maybe," said Duke.

Then Spike said, "Duke, I've been thinking about everything that has happened since I left my milkweed tree and now I'm more confused than ever. I left looking for answers but all I've found is more questions."

"What questions are bothering you?" asked Duke.

Spike sighed and said, "I don't understand why that big duck was afraid of you."

Duke smiled and said, "The duck was afraid of me because of my yellow skin. That's a warning that I'm a poisonous frog."

"Oh," said Spike. "Then why wasn't the snake afraid of you?"

Duke chuckled, "Mr. Snake is as blind as a bat. He depends on his tongue to pick up movement and sound." At that, Spike put one of his little fingers to his chin and looked as though he was deep in thought. Duke smiled at him and asked what was wrong. Spike told him nothing was wrong but then said, "Sue must be super poisonous."

Duke laughed loudly and said, "You're right. Sue's a super girl."

"I hope I don't make you mad," Spike said, "but I have one more question. Why did you run away from Sue before, when now you're stuck on her like glue."

Duke rolled his big eyes around before responding. "I spent my whole life looking at the outside of others," he said. "I judged them by their looks and only learned to look on the inside after Sue saved us from those nasty frogs."

"Does that mean you're not going to run away from Sue again?" Spike asked, smiling.

"You're right, kid," Duke said. "I'm here to stay."

Steven's Big Change

Steven and Psyche were not far away now and, in fact, were closing in on Duke and Spike. Psyche was a little ahead of Steven and had perched on a boulder so that she could wait for him to catch up. That's when she spotted a bright yellow caterpillar lying alongside a frog and knew that she had found Spike and Duke. Overjoyed, she raced back to give Steven the good news. Steven saw her coming towards him faster than he had ever seen her fly before and thought something was chasing her. "What's wrong, Psyche?" he cried.

Psyche stopped right above Steven and fluttered her wings excitedly. "I've found them!" she shrieked.

"What have you found?" Steven shouted back at her.

"Spike and Duke. They're right near here," Psyche replied, turning to go back to where she had discovered the lost friends. But when she looked at Steven, she noticed that he hadn't moved an inch. She flew back over to him and asked, "What's wrong? Aren't you happy to find your friends?"

"What if they don't recognize me?" Steven said worriedly.

"What do you mean? Don't be cute," retorted Psyche.

"You know what I mean," Steven said, lifting one of his webbed feet out of the water.

"Oh. I understand," said Psyche, adding, "You might want to take a little peek at your friends from the boulder first."

Hesitating, Steven said, "Okay, but I'm not going any farther than that."

When Steven reached the boulder, Psyche was already there, of course, perched on top of it. Since Steven's had grown legs, it was now easy for him to climb up next to her. Peering over the boulder, he saw Duke first. All at once it came to him how much he resembled the frog. Turning to Psyche, he said, "I look like Duke."

"Yes, you do," the butterfly smiled.

A little smile formed on Steven's own face and he said, "Now I know what a tadpole becomes."

"Yes," replied Psyche. "A tadpole becomes a frog."

Then Steven noticed a long yellow creature lying beside Duke and asked, "What's that next to Duke?"

Psyche told him, "That's your friend, Spike."

"It doesn't look like him," Steven said.

"I told you before, we all change," Psyche reminded him. "But true friends are friends for life. Come on, let's go. Introduce me."

Steven looked at his friends and then at Psyche and replied, "You're right. Let's go." Then he leapt into the water and began swimming towards Duke and Spike. Up above, Psyche sped past him and settled on an orange pebble right next to Duke and Spike.

"What's that?" shouted Spike, spotting Psyche.

Turning his head to look, Duke whispered, "Quick! It's a butterfly! Make a wish before it flies away."

Spike closed his eyes and wished that he could see Steven again. Almost at once, as if by magic, he heard a familiar voice. Opening his eyes, he said, "Duke, did you hear that?" Duke was staring into the pond, his mouth half open, watching a stream of bubbles shoot up into the sky. Seeing them too, Spike rose up on his hind legs to find out where they were coming from. "Steven," he cried. "Is that you?"

"Yes, it's me!" Steven shouted back.

Spike turned to Duke and said, "Tell me I'm not dreaming."

"You're not dreaming," Duke replied. "It sounds and acts like that little brat."

"Come closer," Spike called to Steven.

"I've changed a lot," Steven warned.

"Haven't we all," Spike sighed.

Steven said, "I'm not kidding. I've really changed and I'm afraid you might not even recognize me."

Duke and Spike glanced at each other, trying to find the right words to say. Psyche broke the silence and told Duke and Spike about how she and Steven had been trying to find them. Then she revealed that Steven had found out first hand what a tadpole becomes. Spike, who had stuck out his black antennae to listen, declared, "That's great!" Then he turned to Steven and said, "Come closer to me so that I can see you or else I'm coming in after you." Without waiting for an answer the caterpillar dove into the water and immediately sank to the bottom. Steven followed him down and, gripping him with his new webbed feet, brought him back up to the surface. He dragged Spike to the edge of the pond and then hopped over to Duke, who couldn't believe his eyes when he saw Steven.

Duke kept opening and closing his eyes as he watched Steven press water out of Spike. When Steven was finished, it was Spike's turn to stare. "Steven, you've become a frog, like Duke," he exclaimed. "That's great!"

Meanwhile, Sue, who had been silent for all this time, croaked so loudly that they all froze. Afterwards, she left the pond and went over to Duke, Steven, Spike and Psyche, who noticed that she had left a stream of tiny eggs behind in the water. Everyone's eyes popped as little tadpoles started chewing their way out of the eggs and soon afterwards began to swim around in circles. Psyche recovered first and said, "Well, Steven, now you know where the eggs come from."

That night, under the stars, the five friends celebrated their discovery way into the night.

46

Spike Finds the Answers

The next morning Spike woke up first and for a change didn't feel hungry. He sensed that something was starting to happen to him and knew he would have to find the answers he was looking for in a hurry. Soon he would begin to build a case around himself and vanish forever. The thought of this made him sad and tearful, and a little envious of Steven, even though he was happy for his friend.

Meanwhile, Psyche had been watching Spike, who thought everyone but him was still asleep. The butterfly sensed Spike's mood and flew from her perch on the duck grass onto a blue pebble that was right beside him. "Good morning," she called out, cheerfully.

Spike lifted his head, dried his eyes and replied, "Good morning." Then he lowered his head again.

"Are you feeling okay?" Psyche asked.

"Yes and no," answered the caterpillar. "I'm really happy for Steven, but I feel sad for myself."

Comforting him, Psyche said, "Everyone has their moments and sometimes others get answers to their questions first." Moving closer, she said, "Who knows, your answers might be right in front of your eyes. If you give up now, you may never find them."

Spike shifted around for a bit, thinking about what the butterfly had said, and then told her, "You're right Psyche. I shouldn't let my emotions stop me from reaching my goal." With that settled, a smile spread across his face.

"Now there's the brave Spike that Steven has described to me," declared Psyche.

Spike and Psyche went to wake the others, so they could all continue the journey to find answers. Steven no longer swam but instead hopped alongside the others, all the while singing his heart out. Psyche managed to get ahead of everyone, as usual, and eventually came upon a milkweed tree that was covered with lots of juicy-looking leaves. She saw caterpillars sprawled all over the tree's branches but noticed that they were making no attempt to eat, even though they were very thin and looked as if they hadn't had a meal in weeks. Curious, Psyche clapped her wings together to get their attention. When all eyes were upon her, she asked one of the caterpillars why no one was eating the tasty-looking leaves. The caterpillar lifted his head and replied weakly, "We're afraid of our skins splitting. We're waiting for Spike to return with the answer to what will happen to us."

It was then that Psyche realized that 'the pond with no end' went around in a circle and that Spike was about to finish up just where he had started out. Smiling, she said, "Your wait for Spike is just about over, because right now he is closer than you think."

With one voice, the caterpillars began shouting, "Where is he? Where is he? We can't wait to see him."

"Have patience my friends," answered Psyche. Then she closed her eyes, folded her wings and, without another word, fell into a deep sleep, ignoring the caterpillars, who were all shouting at her at once. A few yards away, Steven, Duke, Spike and Sue were looking for her, calling her name. Sue spotted the butterfly first and pointed her out to the others. Steven called her name but got no answer.

Meanwhile, Spike was staring at the milkweed tree. Duke noticed him and said, "What's wrong kid?" Spike didn't answer, but instead crawled off Sue's head and inched over to the milkweed tree, as if a magnet were pulling him. Slowly, he began making his way up the stem. Steven was about to hop over to join him when Duke put out a webbed foot and said, "Let him be. His time has come." At that point, Steven realized that Spike was going up to build his case and began to cry.

Spike crawled all the way up the milkweed tree to the big leaf where Psyche was sleeping. As he passed the other caterpillars, they tried to hide. He was now so much bigger than they were that they didn't recognize him and were afraid. Spike shouted, "Don't be afraid! It's me, Spike! I've come back just like I promised!" One by one, the caterpillars began peering out from their hiding places to look at Spike more closely. When they finally recognized him, they jumped up and shouted with joy. "Spike has returned with answers for us!" they cried in chorus.

Spike was about to say something when Psyche opened her eyes, spread her wings and flew off the leaf. There, where she had been lying, was a pile of little eggs. The caterpillars all stared at the eggs in amazement. No one was more stunned than Spike, who stared in disbelief as the eggs hatched and tiny caterpillars crawled out. Smiling down at the little creatures, which wiggled over to him, he said to the other caterpillars, "See, now you know where eggs come from." The caterpillars on the milkweed tree burst into applause. Shyly, Spike backed away, towards the edge of his leaf. But he was heavy now and began to fall. Luckily, a sticky web at the end of his tail attached itself to the leaf and saved him. He began to spin round and round and before long had enclosed himself in a beautiful case that was green with brilliant gold trim.

The caterpillars had watched with alarm as Spike twirled. They realized all too well what was taking place and knew that soon they would have the answer to their biggest question: what happens to caterpillars after they build cases around themselves? Psyche, who had been flying from one milkweed tree to the next laying more eggs, returned to Steven, Duke and Sue and landed on Duke's head. "Don't worry, Spike is going to be fine," she said.

Later on, the day turned into a starless night that eventually became morning. When the sun peeped through the tall trees, the redbird sounded the call that awakened the day creatures. Rising, the caterpillars were surprised to hear noise coming from inside the case that enclosed Spike. Psyche, who woke up well before sunrise, had been waiting impatiently for this to happen. She quickly flew down to wake Duke, Sue and Steven and then pointed to Spike's case. Together they watched as ever so slowly, one at a time, wings began to force their way out of it. "What is going on? What is it?" shouted Steven as Spike emerged and flitted his wings, no longer a caterpillar but now a beautiful butterfly.

Spike looked around at his friends and smiled. Turning to his fellow caterpillars, he said, "Eat and be merry and don't fear your skin splitting. In the end you'll look just like me." The caterpillars called Spike a hero. Then they ate and ate until they couldn't eat any more.

The End

www.ingramcontent.com/pod-product-compliance
Lightning Source LLC
Chambersburg PA
CBHW071145250626
47159CB00006B/2301

* 9 7 8 1 8 9 4 9 1 6 3 9 4 *